THE BOXCAR CHILDREN
SURPRISE ISLAND
THE YELLOW HOUSE MYSTERY
MYSTERY RANCH
MIKE'S MYSTERY
BLUE BAY MYSTERY
THE WOODSHED MYSTERY
THE LIGHTHOUSE MYSTERY
MOUNTAIN TOP MYSTERY
SCHOOLHOUSE MYSTERY
CABOOSE MYSTERY
HOUSEBOAT MYSTERY
SNOWBOUND MYSTERY
TREE HOUSE MYSTERY
BICYCLE MYSTERY
MYSTERY IN THE SAND
MYSTERY BEHIND THE WALL
BUS STATION MYSTERY
BENNY UNCOVERS A MYSTERY
THE HAUNTED CABIN MYSTERY
THE DESERTED LIBRARY MYSTERY
THE ANIMAL SHELTER MYSTERY
THE OLD MOTEL MYSTERY
THE MYSTERY OF THE HIDDEN PAINTING
THE AMUSEMENT PARK MYSTERY
THE MYSTERY OF THE MIXED-UP ZOO
THE CAMP-OUT MYSTERY
THE MYSTERY GIRL
THE MYSTERY CRUISE
THE DISAPPEARING FRIEND MYSTERY
THE MYSTERY OF THE SINGING GHOST
THE MYSTERY IN THE SNOW
THE PIZZA MYSTERY
THE MYSTERY HORSE
THE MYSTERY AT THE DOG SHOW
THE CASTLE MYSTERY
THE MYSTERY OF THE LOST VILLAGE
THE MYSTERY ON THE ICE
THE MYSTERY OF THE PURPLE POOL
THE GHOST SHIP MYSTERY
THE MYSTERY IN WASHINGTON, DC
THE CANOE TRIP MYSTERY
THE MYSTERY OF THE HIDDEN BEACH
THE MYSTERY OF THE MISSING CAT
THE MYSTERY AT SNOWFLAKE INN

THE MYSTERY ON STAGE
THE DINOSAUR MYSTERY
THE MYSTERY OF THE STOLEN MUSIC
THE MYSTERY AT THE BALL PARK
THE CHOCOLATE SUNDAE MYSTERY
THE MYSTERY OF THE HOT AIR BALLOON
THE MYSTERY BOOKSTORE
THE PILGRIM VILLAGE MYSTERY
THE MYSTERY OF THE STOLEN BOXCAR
THE MYSTERY IN THE CAVE
THE MYSTERY ON THE TRAIN
THE MYSTERY AT THE FAIR
THE MYSTERY OF THE LOST MINE
THE GUIDE DOG MYSTERY
THE HURRICANE MYSTERY
THE PET SHOP MYSTERY
THE MYSTERY OF THE SECRET MESSAGE
THE FIREHOUSE MYSTERY
THE MYSTERY IN SAN FRANCISCO
THE NIAGARA FALLS MYSTERY
THE MYSTERY AT THE ALAMO
THE OUTER SPACE MYSTERY
THE SOCCER MYSTERY
THE MYSTERY IN THE OLD ATTIC
THE GROWLING BEAR MYSTERY
THE MYSTERY OF THE LAKE MONSTER
THE MYSTERY AT PEACOCK HALL
THE WINDY CITY MYSTERY
THE BLACK PEARL MYSTERY
THE CEREAL BOX MYSTERY
THE PANTHER MYSTERY
THE MYSTERY OF THE QUEEN'S JEWELS
THE STOLEN SWORD MYSTERY
THE BASKETBALL MYSTERY
THE MOVIE STAR MYSTERY
THE MYSTERY OF THE PIRATE'S MAP
THE GHOST TOWN MYSTERY
THE MYSTERY OF THE BLACK RAVEN
THE MYSTERY IN THE MALL
THE MYSTERY IN NEW YORK
THE GYMNASTICS MYSTERY
THE POISON FROG MYSTERY
THE MYSTERY OF THE EMPTY SAFE
THE HOME RUN MYSTERY
THE GREAT BICYCLE RACE MYSTERY

THE MYSTERY OF THE WILD PONIES
THE MYSTERY IN THE COMPUTER GAME
THE HONEYBEE MYSTERY
THE MYSTERY AT THE CROOKED HOUSE
THE HOCKEY MYSTERY
THE MYSTERY OF THE MIDNIGHT DOG
THE MYSTERY OF THE SCREECH OWL
THE SUMMER CAMP MYSTERY
THE COPYCAT MYSTERY
THE HAUNTED CLOCK TOWER MYSTERY
THE MYSTERY OF THE TIGER'S EYE
THE DISAPPEARING STAIRCASE MYSTERY
THE MYSTERY ON BLIZZARD MOUNTAIN
THE MYSTERY OF THE SPIDER'S CLUE
THE CANDY FACTORY MYSTERY
THE MYSTERY OF THE MUMMY'S CURSE
THE MYSTERY OF THE STAR RUBY
THE STUFFED BEAR MYSTERY
THE MYSTERY OF ALLIGATOR SWAMP
THE MYSTERY AT SKELETON POINT
THE TATTLETALE MYSTERY
THE COMIC BOOK MYSTERY
THE GREAT SHARK MYSTERY
THE ICE CREAM MYSTERY
THE MIDNIGHT MYSTERY
THE MYSTERY IN THE FORTUNE COOKIE
THE BLACK WIDOW SPIDER MYSTERY
THE RADIO MYSTERY
THE MYSTERY OF THE RUNAWAY GHOST
THE FINDERS KEEPERS MYSTERY
THE MYSTERY OF THE HAUNTED BOXCAR
THE CLUE IN THE CORN MAZE
THE GHOST OF THE CHATTERING BONES
THE SWORD OF THE SILVER KNIGHT
THE GAME STORE MYSTERY
THE MYSTERY OF THE ORPHAN TRAIN
THE VANISHING PASSENGER
THE GIANT YO-YO MYSTERY
THE CREATURE IN OGOPOGO LAKE
THE ROCK 'N' ROLL MYSTERY
THE SECRET OF THE MASK
THE SEATTLE PUZZLE
THE GHOST IN THE FIRST ROW
THE BOX THAT WATCH FOUND
A HORSE NAMED DRAGON

THE GREAT DETECTIVE RACE
THE GHOST AT THE DRIVE-IN MOVIE
THE MYSTERY OF THE TRAVELING TOMATOES
THE SPY GAME
THE DOG-GONE MYSTERY
THE VAMPIRE MYSTERY
SUPERSTAR WATCH
THE SPY IN THE BLEACHERS
THE AMAZING MYSTERY SHOW
THE PUMPKIN HEAD MYSTERY
THE CUPCAKE CAPER
THE CLUE IN THE RECYCLING BIN
MONKEY TROUBLE
THE ZOMBIE PROJECT
THE GREAT TURKEY HEIST
THE GARDEN THIEF
THE BOARDWALK MYSTERY
THE MYSTERY OF THE FALLEN TREASURE
THE RETURN OF THE GRAVEYARD GHOST
THE MYSTERY OF THE STOLEN SNOWBOARD
THE MYSTERY OF THE WILD WEST BANDIT
THE MYSTERY OF THE SOCCER SNITCH
THE MYSTERY OF THE GRINNING GARGOYLE
THE MYSTERY OF THE MISSING POP IDOL
THE MYSTERY OF THE STOLEN DINOSAUR BONES
THE MYSTERY AT THE CALGARY STAMPEDE
THE SLEEPY HOLLOW MYSTERY
THE LEGEND OF THE IRISH CASTLE
THE CELEBRITY CAT CAPER
HIDDEN IN THE HAUNTED SCHOOL
THE ELECTION DAY DILEMMA
JOURNEY ON A RUNAWAY TRAIN
THE CLUE IN THE PAPYRUS SCROLL
THE DETOUR OF THE ELEPHANTS
THE SHACKLETON SABOTAGE
THE KHIPU AND THE FINAL KEY
THE DOUGHNUT WHODUNIT
THE ROBOT RANSOM
NEW! THE LEGEND OF THE HOWLING WEREWOLF
NEW! THE DAY OF THE DEAD MYSTERY

THE BOXCAR CHILDREN®

CREATED BY
GERTRUDE CHANDLER WARNER

BOOK

148

THE LEGEND OF THE HOWLING WEREWOLF

ILLUSTRATED BY
ANTHONY VanARSDALE

ALBERT WHITMAN & COMPANY
CHICAGO, ILLINOIS

Copyright © 2018 by Albert Whitman & Company
First published in the United States of America
in 2018 by Albert Whitman & Company

ISBN 978-0-8075-0740-7 (hardcover)
ISBN 978-0-8075-0741-4 (paperback)

Printed in the United States of America
10 9 8 7 6 5 4 3 2 1 LB 22 21 20 19 18

Illustrations by Anthony VanArsdale

Visit the Boxcar Children online at www.boxcarchildren.com.
For more information about Albert Whitman & Company,
visit our website at www.albertwhitman.com.

Contents

A Strange Rumor

Grandfather Alden pulled his rental car onto the interstate. He looked over his left shoulder, waiting for traffic to pass. Then he sped up. "Couple more hours until we get to Mrs. Riley's house," he told his four grandchildren.

Ten-year-old Violet was in the backseat. Her pigtails bounced as she turned to see the road signs. "'Welcome to Idaho,'" she read aloud. Another sign whizzed by. "Famous Potatoes.'"

"'Where are all the potatoes, Grandfather?" she asked.

He nodded toward the windows. "See all those bare fields out there? Desert, really. Miles and miles of crops have already been harvested. It's

October, so potatoes are being sent to all parts of the country by train and truck."

"For French fries and hash browns, right, Grandfather?" six-year-old Benny, who was sitting next to Violet, said.

Grandfather smiled at Benny in his rearview mirror. "That's right," he said. "When we get to Townsend, you'll see that sugar beets are another important crop in Idaho. They're part of a fun event this weekend."

"That's exciting," said Benny. "When will we get there?"

"Soon," said Grandfather for the fifth time that hour. "Try to enjoy the view, Benny. Do you know those mountains in the distance?"

"Uh, no, not really," Benny said. He looked to his brother in the front seat for an answer.

"Those are the Rockies," said fourteen-year-old Henry. "They go all the way from Canada down to New Mexico. They'll be covered with snow all winter."

After a while, they passed some hills with steep sides and flat tops.

"They look like tables," said Jessie.

"Those are called buttes," Grandfather explained. "They are actually volcanic cones. See their black sides?"

"Lava!" said Henry. "We studied buttes in science class. Volcanoes used to bubble up here. And when the lava dried, it made the buttes. But I think these volcanoes have sleeping for a long time."

"That's right, Henry," said Grandfather.

"What if they wake up while we're here?" asked Violet.

"The last eruption was about two thousand years ago," Grandfather said. "No need to worry. And here we are." He slowed the car, clicked on his turn signal, and took the exit.

"Look, Benny, we're almost there," said Henry. He pointed to a sign out the window.

"'Welcome to Townsend. Home of the Sage Hen,'" Benny read slowly. "What's that mean, Grandfather?"

"It looks like a chicken," said Violet, who was looking at the bird shown on the sign.

"It does, I suppose," Grandfather said with a

chuckle. "Sage hens are also called sage grouse. Strange creatures. The males do this funny dance to attract the females. It's quite the sight. That's one reason a lot of tourists come to up to places like Townsend."

"I hope we can get a close look," said Jessie. "And I want to see some lava." She was twelve, and she loved animals. She rolled down the window for her dog, Watch, so he could sniff the cool autumn air.

"I hope we see them too," said Henry. As the oldest, he liked to take charge. "Maybe I can lead us all on a hike. And hopefully we'll come across an old volcano."

"You'll have plenty of time to explore in the next few days," said Grandfather. "When I was a boy, I went to summer camp here. The area is rich in geology and Native American history."

As Grandfather drove down Main Street, he said, "I'm excited for you to meet my friend Mrs. Riley. She has a big project I think will interest you all."

"I can't wait to meet her," said Jessie.

Violet looked over at her grandfather. "We love projects!"

"Yes, I know, dear." Grandfather gave her a friendly wink.

The Alden children were orphans. After their parents died, they had learned they must go live with a grandfather they had never met. They heard he was mean, so they ran away to the woods, where they found shelter in an old boxcar. That's where they found their wire fox terrier, Watch. Soon their grandfather found them. He wasn't mean at all! He brought them to his home in Greenfield, Connecticut, to live as a family. He even had the boxcar brought to his backyard. Now the Aldens used it as their clubhouse.

Grandfather traveled often. When possible, he brought his grandchildren with him so they would have new experiences. This trip had brought him to Boise, Idaho. And now he and the children were on their way across the state to visit his friend Mrs. Riley.

***

Trees along Townsend's Main Street were gold and crimson with fall leaves. Grandfather turned up a gravel driveway just outside of town. A single-story ranch house sat in a field of sagebrush. Wide windows faced the foothills of the mountains.

A woman in jeans and a plaid shirt came from the front porch to greet the Aldens. Her long dark hair hung in a braid over her shoulder. She wore turquoise earrings and a turquoise bracelet. She shook hands with Grandfather and smiled at the children. "I'm Susan Riley," she told them. "I'm very happy to meet you. And James, it's wonderful to see you again."

"Thank you for inviting us, Susan," said Grandfather.

She turned to the children. "This is a good weekend to be here, because it's our very first Harvest Festival. I'm on the City Council and am one of the festival organizers."

"That sounds like fun," said Jessie. "Do you need any help?"

"Actually, yes," the woman said. "There is much to do, and it would be nice to have some help. Would that interest you?"

"Yes!" Violet replied quickly.

"I love to help," Benny said.

"We all do," Jessie said. "The middle school Henry and I go to will give us extra credit for community service. But even if they didn't, we would still want to help you."

"That's right," Henry agreed.

"Well come on in," Mrs. Riley said. "I've set out some snacks in case anyone's hungry."

Benny's face lit up. His family laughed. "Benny's always hungry," Jessie explained.

"Then you're in the right place," their hostess said. She waved them inside, and they went to the kitchen. A table in the center of the room had plates of sliced apples, cheese, and crackers. "Sit, please," she said, pouring each child a glass of milk. She brought Grandfather a steaming mug of tea. Watch curled up under the table, waiting for any dropped food.

"What is the Harvest Festival?" Benny asked. "Is it for the potatoes your town planted?"

"Good question, Benny," the woman replied. "Idaho certainly is famous for potatoes, but the big crop around Townsend is sugar beets."

"Sugar beets?" Jessie said. "Do people make a

pie or cake with those?"

"In a way, yes," Mrs. Riley said. "But first the beets are sent to factories. They're processed into the type of sugar used for baking. Soda companies also use it to sweeten soft drinks."

"But can you eat a sugar beet like one of these apples?" Benny asked.

Mrs. Riley laughed. "I'll let you find out tomorrow, Benny. Meanwhile, I'll show you all to where you are staying so you can settle in."

When the children were done eating, they took their plates to the sink. Then they went and got their bags from the car. After picking where they would sleep, they joined Grandfather and Mrs. Riley on the back deck. She was looking at the foothills, now golden in the afternoon sun.

"Are there any sage grouse out there?" Henry asked.

"Probably," she replied. "Not only are they becoming rare, but they're hard to spot. Their feathers are camouflaged in the brush."

Jessie opened her notebook and clicked her pen. "Mrs. Riley, what do you need help with to get ready for the Harvest Festival? Just tell us, and we'll get started."

"That's very kind, Jessie. Thank you." Mrs. Riley continued to stare at the hills. "Something's been troubling me though."

"What is it, Susan?" Grandfather asked.

She sighed. "I'm worried no one will show up on Sunday. Especially for the evening parade."

"Why is that?" asked Henry.

"For the past few months, a rumor has been going around town," Mrs. Riley said. "A strange and upsetting rumor."

The Alden children exchanged glances. They looked at their host with concern.

"What rumor?" Violet asked. She suddenly felt cold and rubbed her arms to warm up.

Mrs. Riley motioned toward the foothills. "Someone posted on our website that a werewolf lives up there," she said.

Benny gulped. He said, "A werewolf?"

Mrs. Riley nodded. "Yes," she said. "And when the harvest moon gets full, as it will this weekend, the creature supposedly sneaks into town. Some people are afraid of going outside."

The children were quiet for a moment. Then Henry said, "But there's no such thing as a werewolf. Isn't that right, Grandfather?"

"I'm certain they don't exist," said Grandfather.

Violet looked up at Grandfather. In a quiet voice she said, "But what if they do exist?"

CHAPTER 2

Sounds in the Night

As the sun set, Mrs. Riley led the Aldens back into the house. She invited them to hang their sweatshirts on the rack by her back door. The kitchen was cozy from the warm stove.

"I'll show you what has caused such alarm," she said. She brought her laptop to the kitchen table and sat on one of the bench seats. After a few clicks, a cheerful photo of jack-o'-lanterns appeared on the screen. She scrolled down and paused at a video of dancing sage grouse.

"These are the birds that made our town famous," she explained. "I'm from the Shoshone-Bannock tribe. Our elders tell stories about long ago. There were thousands of these birds. They darkened the sky when they took flight. The sound of their wings was like wind. Can you imagine?"

"It must have been quite a sight," Grandfather said.

"Oh, yes, I wish we could have witnessed it," Mrs. Riley said. "Anyway, this is the website I created with Mayor Chang. You'll meet her this weekend, children. Here we are. But look at this upsetting rumor." She scrolled down to the comments.

Benny leaned close. "I think I can read this," he said.

"Go for it," Mrs. Riley said. She scooted along the bench so Benny could sit beside her. The others stood close enough to see for themselves.

"'Beware...Danger,'" Benny began, sounding out the words. His eyes grew wide. "Are we in danger?"

"I sure hope not," Henry said. He peered at the screen and continued reading. "'A mysterious event has occurred over the past months during each full moon. In the middle of the night, a person has been seen dashing along the ridge that overlooks town. Then, at the break in the trees, the moonlight is bright.'"

Henry exchanged a worried look with Jessie. "This is spooky," she said. She stood behind her brother and looked over his shoulder. "'In the moonlight,'" Jessie read, "'the figure bends down. And after a moment, it lets out a whimper, like a groan. When the figure stands back up, it has the head of a wolf, and it staggers until it is out of sight.'"

Benny went to the kitchen window and looked out into the night. Turning back to his family he said, "A real werewolf? I hope we see it!"

"Let's check the other comments," said Henry. He scrolled down and kept reading. "'Whoever the werewolf is, he or she hikes into the foothills before the moon rises, to transform in secret. Then during daylight, the shape-shifter comes back to town like a normal person who lives here. As if nothing happened.'"

"But werewolves are just a myth," said Jessie.

"That's right," said Grandfather. "Legends of werewolves have been around for a very long time. People use them to try to explain things they don't understand. But there has never been anything to suggest that werewolves actually exist."

A ding came from the computer. There was a new comment on the website. "Uh-oh," Violet said. "Mrs. Riley, this person says the festival must be canceled immediately. 'The threat of the werewolf is even greater during a harvest moon.'"

"This is what worries me," Mrs. Riley said. "People checking the website are going to see this. It would be terrible if it kept families from enjoying a fun weekend. Mayor Chang and I were hoping the festival would bring more tourists to our community."

Henry noticed the motel and restaurant ads on the website. "I get it now," he said. "Visitors will spend money while they're here. It will help Townsend."

"You're exactly right, Henry," Mrs. Riley said.

"If tourists are afraid to come," Henry added, "it will hurt the town."

"Right again," Mrs. Riley said. She went to the pantry and pulled out things for dinner. She handed Grandfather six salad bowls for the table. "I don't know about you folks, but all this worrying makes me hungry," she said.

"Me too!" shouted Benny.

While their host prepared dinner, the children set the table. They poured glasses of water. As Jessie folded a paper napkin by each plate, she paused to look up. "Mrs. Riley," she said, "I'm curious. What is a harvest moon?"

"Is it different than a regular moon?" Benny asked.

"And what does it have to do with werewolves?" Violet asked.

Henry said, "It sounds like someone is trying to sabotage the festival, Mrs. Riley. I wonder why."

Mrs. Riley gave the children a caring look. Then she turned to Grandfather and said, "I really like how your grandchildren think about things and ask questions. You must be very proud of them, James."

He smiled. "I certainly am."

"All right then," said Mrs. Riley. "A harvest moon happens in the fall, during something called the autumnal equinox. For several nights in a row, the moon rises near sunset. Those nights are extra bright, because it seems like there are full moons multiple nights in a row."

The Alden children listened with interest.

Mrs. Riley explained further. "Here in Idaho an abundance of moonlight right after sunset helps farmers harvest the summer crops. It's a nice boost before winter snows arrive."

The good aromas of dinner filled the warm kitchen. "Almost ready," Mrs. Riley said. She gave Henry a big bowl of salad and a bottle of dressing to put on the table. "Any more questions before we dig in?"

Benny raised his hand like he was in school. "Are there wolves around here?" he asked. "I mean real ones."

"They are in more mountainous country," she said. "We have coyotes, but they tend to stay away from town. They sound different too. Coyotes yip in high voices. Wolves howl."

"Do they scare you?" Jessie asked.

"Sometimes, yes," she answered. "Their cries sound haunting. But wolves and other scavengers are our friends. They clean up the desert. They keep the deer population from getting too big.

That means there are more flowers and brush for smaller animals to eat. Are you kids worried?"

The children shook their heads.

"That's good," Mrs. Riley said. She pulled a casserole from the oven. She set it on the table with a large serving spoon. "Here you go, everyone. I'm glad you're here."

***

That night the children woke to a noise outside their window. Something was rustling and snapping twigs.

"Shhh," Henry whispered. He shined his flashlight around the den where they had unrolled their sleeping bags.

"Maybe it's the werewolf," Benny whispered. "Let's go look. Watch will protect us."

"Benny, there's no such thing," said Jessie.

Quietly the children slipped on their shoes and socks. They tiptoed down the hallway and paused at the great room, where Grandfather slept on a foldout couch. He was snoring loudly.

Jessie put her finger to her lips. They passed Mrs. Riley's room. Even Watch was quiet, though he wagged his tail, excited for an adventure. His ears were alert.

In the kitchen, the children zipped on their sweatshirts over their pajamas. The door creaked as they let themselves outside. Their breaths made frost in the cold night air. Moonlight spread over the mountains.

"It's so bright out," Henry said. He barely needed his flashlight to see. But he kept it on just in case.

The children crept along a path that led to a field. At the edge of the yard, they looked back at the house. The windows were dark except for a tiny glow from the kitchen clock. "Everyone's still asleep," said Jessie. "Let's be careful. Benny, stay close to me, please. I don't want you to stumble."

Benny grabbed Jessie's free hand. She held Watch's leash with the other. The terrier wiggled and lunged forward. He seemed to smell something up ahead. Henry led the way with Violet hiding behind him. The children stepped cautiously up the hill.

Suddenly Watch began a low growl. He cocked his head, listening, then pulled at his leash again.

Sounds in the Night

Sounds of scurrying and scratching came from within clumps of sagebrush.

Just as Henry bent down to look, a thunder of beating wings came from the bushes. The children jumped back, and a bird with a puffy white chest fluttered up and away. Then two more followed it into the moonlit sky.

Watch barked and started to run after the birds. Jessie held tight to his collar. "No, boy," she said. "We don't want you to hurt them."

The children were quiet for a moment as the birds flew away.

Then Violet said, "Those birds looked like the ones we saw on the sign coming into town. With the same pointed tail feathers."

"I guess we just saw our first sage grouse," Henry said. "Up close and personal."

Jessie looked toward the dark house. "We better get back," she said, "before Grandfather wakes up and worries about us. Plus, I feel weird that we're walking around in our pj's."

Benny sighed. In the moonlight the others could see his frown. "You look disappointed," Henry said.

"I was hoping we'd see the werewolf," Benny said.

"Maybe we'll find more clues tomorrow," Henry said. "And maybe we'll see a sleeping volcano. Would you like that?"

Benny grinned.

Back in the kitchen the children hung up their sweatshirts. They got drinks of water and brushed their teeth, because they'd forgotten to earlier. At last they settled into their sleeping bags. The room was dark, except for moonlight shining through a window. It made a patch of square light on the floor.

"I can't sleep," said Jessie.

"I'm wide awake," said Benny. Just for fun, he shined his flashlight around the room, making scary shadows.

Violet lay with her eyes open. She was still tense from seeing the sage grouse fly out of the bushes. "What if there really is a werewolf?" she asked.

"Don't worry, Violet," said Henry. "Even if there were, we'd be safe with Grandfather and Mrs. Riley. And besides, Watch won't let anything happen to us."

Sounds in the Night

At the sound of his name, Watch lifted his head. Violet stroked his back to calm him down, and before long they were both fast asleep.

CHAPTER 3

Odd Shoes

The next morning the children found a note on the kitchen table. "Help yourselves to cereal, toast, and fruit," Mrs. Riley had written. "Your grandfather and I will be at the festival grounds. Come join us. It's just a few blocks away." She had drawn a map.

After clearing their breakfast dishes, the Aldens grabbed their daypacks. Prepared for a long day, they brought sweatshirts and water bottles. Jessie liked to have her notebook and pen handy. She also carried a little bag of doggie treats. Violet brought her camera. Its strap was purple, her favorite color. As the children walked toward town, Watch trotted ahead, his head high. The terrier was energized by the cool autumn air.

Odd Shoes

Along the way, they passed a row of cottages. One of the yards had the remains of a summer garden. Squash and green beans hung from a trellis with small pumpkins. A man was clipping the yellowed vines and filling a wheelbarrow when he saw the children. He was tall and skinny with dark skin and black hair.

"Hello, there," he said. "You're visiting, right? My name is Daniel."

The Aldens introduced themselves. Benny said, "We have a garden like yours at home. Do you need any help?"

"That's nice of you to offer," Daniel said, "but no thanks. I'm almost done here. Say, I heard you kids had a run-in last night with some sage grouse."

The children glanced at one another. "How did you know that?" Henry asked.

"Mrs. Riley told me earlier this morning," Daniel answered. "Whenever she drives by, she rolls down her window to say hello. We're old friends."

Again the children exchanged glances. "But we never told Mrs. Riley," said Jessie. "We didn't even tell our grandfather."

Daniel went over to his pumpkins. He began twisting the ripe ones from their stems and putting them in a basket. He avoided looking at the children.

Henry waited for an explanation, but then spoke up. "How did you find out about last night?" he asked.

Finally Daniel faced the children. "All right, all right," he said. "I'm a biologist. I love the beauty and wild nature of the sage grouse, especially in the moonlight. Anyway, last night I was out walking."

"Is that when you saw us?" Violet said.

"Yes," Daniel said. "When your dog growled, the birds flew out of the bushes. I rushed over to look. It's not often we see them around here anymore."

"Why is that?" Benny asked.

Daniel pointed to an empty lot down the street. A rumbling tractor was plowing up the dirt. "See over there?" he said. "People are moving to Townsend because it's so peaceful here. They build new homes and mini farms. But the noise they create scares away the deer and elk. The torn-up soil destroys dens for the pygmy rabbits. It chases voles into our neighborhoods."

"Do you mean moles?" Benny asked.

"Not quite," Daniel said. "Moles eat insects, like worms. Voles are much smaller and look like mice. They eat seeds and the roots of flowers and vegetables. They practically destroyed my garden last year. I don't mind if voles stay out in the wild."

"So the bulldozers are messing up the habitat?" Henry said. "That's sad."

"Yes, it is," Daniel said. "That's why the sage grouse are disappearing. The vegetation is important for their survival. Songbirds also use the branches for nesting. As you can guess, cement driveways and patios cover up the sagebrush. Forever."

"I feel sorry for the animals," Jessie said. "Especially the little ones."

"So do I." Daniel continued talking to them as he pushed his wheelbarrow to a compost pile. He tipped it to dump out the twigs and leaves he had clipped. "The city council wants to devote more land to new housing and to farmers," he said. "Our town is struggling financially, so this would bring in more money. But that means more noisy equipment and plowed earth. These developments will destroy brush that shelters the beautiful grouse. Maybe you've noticed our street signs have symbols of these birds?"

The children nodded. They had noticed them when they came into town the day before.

"I'm sorry to go on and on," Daniel said. "I'm just frustrated. Some of the people around here call me a conservationist, like it's a bad thing. But it's not."

"What's a conservationist?" Benny asked.

"Someone who tries to protect the environment," Violet answered. "Like the forests and the animals, even the desert."

"Take this chicken coop for instance," Daniel said. He walked over to a big pen on wheels. Clucking hens and chicks scurried inside as he rolled the pen to a fresh patch of grass. "I don't use chemicals or pesticides. These free-range chickens lay beautiful, healthy eggs."

"That is really cool," Jessie said.

"I'm glad you think so too," Daniel said. "Well, it's been nice talking to you kids. Time to get back to my chores. See you around."

The children walked on. Violet said, "Daniel

seems to really care about animals."

"He does," Henry said. "But it is strange that he was out last night."

"Oh! I have an idea," said Benny. "What if Daniel is the werewolf? What if he was out hunting for a snack last night, like a sage grouse?"

"There is no such thing as werewolves, Benny," said Jessie. "Maybe he really was studying the birds when he spotted us."

Benny crossed his arms. "I still think my idea is good," he said.

"It is strange that he lied about seeing us," said Henry. "Why would he do that?"

The children stopped in the road to look back at Daniel. He was bent over pushing his wheelbarrow.

"That's a really good question," said Jessie, writing in her notebook. "We need to figure out why."

***

The Aldens arrived at a large park with picnic tables and a playground. Grandfather was hammering a sign into the dirt. It said Harvest Festival This Weekend. Everyone Welcome.

The Legend of the Howling Werewolf

"Hello, children," Grandfather said. "You're just in time. Henry, you're good at fixing things." Grandfather nodded toward a puddle of mud below a leaky water fountain. "I can't seem to stop the dripping."

Henry leaned down to look at the problem. "Oh, it's the faucet," he said. "It just needs a new washer. Where can I find some tools?"

"Check over there," Grandfather said. He motioned toward a table with a toolbox and some art supplies on it.

While Henry worked on the fountain, the others explored the park. Nearby, a freshly painted poster glistened in the sunlight. The letters were still wet: Fun Run—Start Here. A woman in jogging pants and a slim shirt was unwinding a rope of flags. A big gray and white dog lay in the grass beside her. He was on a leash. But when Watch came wagging up to the dog, it growled. It lunged at Watch, barking and barking.

"No, Kamu, no!" the woman said.

"Is he dangerous?" Benny asked.

"Not at all," the woman said. "Kamu is really

quite sweet, but he is very protective of me. I'm terribly sorry he startled you. I'm Ellen, by the way."

The Aldens told Ellen their names. Violet said, "Our grandfather is putting up signs. Is there anything we can help you with?"

"Actually, yes," Ellen said. "I'm organizing a fun run. Here, Benny, you can take this end of the rope. We need to make the finish line."

"I'm on it!" Benny said.

"And here you go, girls." Ellen handed Violet and Jessie two poles with yellow flags. "The finish line is over there, by the volleyball nets. Just plant them in the sand."

"Okay. First, can I give Kamu a little treat?" Jessie asked. She loved meeting other people's pets.

"Sure. I appreciate you asking. Here, Kamu, sit." Ellen unclipped his leash. With a cautious step, he ambled over to Watch. Then came friendly, wagging tails as Kamu and Watch touched noses.

"They like each other!" Benny said.

"Sometimes it takes a while," Ellen said. "He was rescued from the dog pound. He's a malamute. This summer, campers found him by Lost River, soaking wet and scared."

"Oh, Kamu," the children said, bending down to pet him.

"I think that's why he's so timid," Ellen said. "Even though malamutes are a courageous breed, Kamu's afraid to get his paws wet. We think he almost drowned in the river."

"That would make me afraid," said Jessie.

"Watch was a lost dog too," Benny said. "When we first saw him he was limping. Jessie found a thorn in his paw and pulled it out."

While petting Kamu, Violet noticed Ellen's shoes. They looked like gloves. There was a place for each toe. "I've never seen shoes like that before," she said. "Are they slippers?"

Ellen smiled. "I know. They are odd looking. They're called toe shoes," she said. "I bought them at the running store. They're more comfortable than my sneakers and weigh less. It's like going barefoot, but with more protection."

Violet reached in her pack for her camera. "Is it okay if I get some pictures?"

"You bet." Ellen pointed her feet like a ballerina

then leapt forward like she was running.

Violet took several photos. "I'm doing a school project about our weekend here," she said. "Thank you."

"You're welcome, Violet. And thanks everyone for your help." Ellen went to the fountain to fill Kamu's water bowl. He followed her, but started whimpering. His tail went between his legs.

"Oh, Kamu," said Ellen. "Don't worry." She gently took his collar and led him around the muddy area. She set his bowl in the grass so he could drink. "See what I mean?" she said to the Aldens. "Sometimes I forget how nervous he is around water, even puddles."

The children watched Ellen jog through the park with Kamu. The dog kept glancing up at her. He seemed reassured to be running on the dry path.

Benny crossed his arms with a serious look.

"What're you thinking about, Benny?" Henry asked.

"I'm thinking Kamu might be the werewolf," said Benny. "He's huge! Or maybe he's a werewolf's best friend."

Odd Shoes

"I don't think so," Jessie said. She and Violet laughed kindly.

Henry ruffled his little brother's hair. "Remember, Benny?" he said. "Werewolves are only a myth. There has to be another explanation for what's going on around here."

4

Claw Marks

Falling leaves dropped a patchwork of colors throughout the park. As the Alden children explored the festival grounds, they scuffed and crunched through the leaves. They kicked them in the air, laughing. They scooped them up and tossed armfuls to one another.

"These would be great for an art project," Violet yelled.

"There are even some purples," said her sister. "Your favorite."

They came to an old farm wagon where Mrs. Riley was unloading decorations. She gave them a friendly wave. "I so appreciate you all helping," she said.

"You're welcome, Mrs. Riley," Henry said. "Just show us where to start."

"Okay," she said. "You'll find some hay bales in the barn. They're quite heavy but are on a cart you can roll out here. We can use them for extra seating near the picnic tables. We're going to have a contest there."

"We love contests. What kind?" Violet asked.

"Carving jack-o'-lanterns from sugar beets. Yes. Sugar beets," she said when she saw their surprised faces.

"Like pumpkins at Halloween?" Benny asked.

"Exactly," Mrs. Riley said. "It's a local tradition. And a lot of fun because sugar beets have so many interesting shapes. I'm expecting a good turnout this afternoon."

"I thought the festival wasn't for two days," Jessie said.

"That is when everything will be judged," Mrs. Riley said. "We decided it was best to hold the competitions beforehand. There's less pressure on everyone that way. "

"What else can we do?" Jessie asked.

"The sugar beets are also in the barn," said Mrs. Riley. "Can you also bring them out here?"

"Yes!" Benny replied eagerly.

The Aldens and Watch followed a path to the large, red barn. It was being used as a maintenance shed for the park. When the children stepped inside, they could hear the cooing of pigeons high in the rafters. Tall rows of windows were gray with dust. It took a moment for the children's eyes to adjust to the dim light.

Soon they were able to see. But when they looked around, Jessie gasped. "Oh no," she said. "What happened in here?"

"This doesn't seem right," Violet said. She got out her camera to take pictures.

Smashed sugar beets and pumpkins littered the floor. Their stringy insides oozed into the dirt. Bales of hay had been ripped open. Straw was strewn around like confetti. Brochures for the event had been ripped into shreds.

"What a mess," Henry said. "It looks like someone is trying to sabotage the weekend." He walked around the piles of debris. Watch followed him, sniffing the ruins. "I wonder who did this."

"Maybe the people posting on the website?" Violet asked.

Henry continued to study the damage. "Could be," he said. "They might think a werewolf will sneak into the park and hurt someone."

"Boy, Mrs. Riley is going to be upset," Benny said.

Jessie looked up at the rafters. "Someone wrecked all these decorations so the festival will be canceled? So if no one's out here on the harvest moon," she continued, "no one will get hurt?"

"Sounds about right," her older brother said. "If we're going to help Mrs. Riley, we need to prove there's no such thing as a werewolf. And do it fast."

"Let's tell her what happened," said Jessie. But they were interrupted by a shout.

"Hey everyone," Benny yelled. "I know who did this! Come look." He had wandered to an empty horse stall and was looking at a pile of loose hay. The wire strap that had held the bale together had been cut. He poked a stick at it and looked at the dirt underneath. "The werewolf has been here!" he cried.

The others hurried over. "Werewolf?" Violet asked. "What do you mean, Benny?"

"Right here. See?" Benny knelt down, pointing his stick. Something had clawed the hay and clawed the dirt. The marks were deep. Each had five rows, like long fingers. Benny showed them the smashed sugar beets. Their tough shells also had these marks.

"See?" Benny said.

The children stared wide-eyed at his discovery. Watch sat on Benny's foot, as he often did during a serious discussion. The terrier seemed to be listening carefully.

"Hmm," Henry finally said. "I agree this is weird."

"Wait a second," Jessie said. "Even if these are claw marks, wouldn't a werewolf rather hunt animals? Like sage grouse? Why would it sneak into this barn and wreck stuff?"

"To make sure the festival is canceled," someone behind them said. A badge on the man's vest read *Volunteer*. He had stepped into the barn when he heard the children's voices. "I saw the website. Werewolves come to life during the harvest moon.

They're dangerous. Someone just wants to keep people home where it's safe."

Before the children could respond, the man hurried away. In the parking lot, he spoke to other volunteers who had just arrived. One by one they drove off.

Mrs. Riley noticed them leaving. She rushed to the barn. "What's happening?" she cried.

When the children showed her what had happened, Mrs. Riley stared in disbelief. "I don't understand why someone wants to sabotage everything," she said. "The festival would be fun for families. And good for the community. What a mystery this has become."

At the word mystery, the Alden children gave one another knowing looks. "We'll try to help you figure things out," Jessie offered.

Mrs. Riley smiled. "Thank you. But at the moment I'm not sure what to do," she said.

Henry said, "At least we can help clean up."

"And we'll rescue what's left of the sugar beets," Violet added.

The children found a tarp covering a woodpile.

They pulled it off and shook the dirt out of it. After spreading it on the barn floor, they filled it with bumpy brown beets. Then they each grabbed a corner and with shuffling steps carried it out into the sunshine.

"Oof, this is heavy!" Jessie groaned.

"Ugh, sure is," Henry said.

"Over here!" Mrs. Riley waved them to one of the long tables. "Thank you," she said. "I feel we should carry on with the festival despite this damage. So please arrange them here, and people can choose the one they want to carve. Do any of you like to draw?"

Violet answered by holding up colored markers from the art box.

"Oh good," Mrs. Riley said. "Here's some poster board. It's to announce the contests. Your grandfather is at the store buying award ribbons."

On the poster Violet and Benny drew sugar beet jack-o'-lanterns with grinning faces. They added curlicues and pine trees. They glued assorted leaves onto the edges then wrote in big letters: Harvest Festival Contests Begin at 1:00 p.m.

Today. All Are Welcome.

"Beautiful, you two. Thank you," Mrs. Riley said. Then she went to hang up the sign at the park entrance.

The Alden children returned to the barn. They found a broom and shovels. They scooped up the smashed beets into a barrel with a green lid. The lid said: Compost, Vegetable Matter Only.

"It's for recycling," Henry reminded the others. "The barrel with the blue lid is for paper and aluminum cans."

"I'll sweep up the paper," Violet volunteered.

Benny found a rake to gather up the loose hay. While making a pile near the horse stable, he bent down to look at the dirt. "Uh-oh," he said, loud enough for the others to hear.

"What's the matter, Benny? Are you okay?" Henry asked.

"I think I made a mistake," he answered.

Henry hurried over with his sisters. "What kind of mistake, Benny?" Jessie said.

Benny dragged the rake toward his feet. It made five deep marks in the dirt. Then he raked the dirt alongside the claw marks from earlier. He sighed. "They're the same," he said. "I guess the werewolf hasn't been here after all."

Henry put his hand on Benny's shoulder. "It's okay," he said. "You made a smart observation, Benny. Now let's go have some fun."

The Aldens ate bagged lunches Grandfather had prepared for them, and soon after they were done, groups of people started arriving for the carving competition. Sugar beets ranged from the size of a tennis ball to a tall cookie jar. There were plenty of carving tools and spoons for scooping out seeds. There were magic markers, glue, and scissors.

Violet chose a tall, narrow beet that was a little crooked at the top. She carved out two eyes, a nose, and a goofy smile. She glued purple leaves on each side of its head for ears. Then she pasted yellow leaves around the top, as if they were a golden crown. Benny, Jessie, and Henry chose beets the size of bumpy cantaloupes. Their carvings were equally cheerful.

"We'll put candles in them this evening," said

Mrs. Riley. She looked at the tables where kids were still decorating jack-o'-lanterns. "I just hope no one comes and destroys these beautiful works of art."

***

After the children were done helping out at the competitions, they headed back to Mrs. Riley's house. Daniel was not in his yard when they passed his place. His wheelbarrow lay on its side with branches and twigs spilled out onto the ground. A bag of soil had been ripped open.

"That's weird," Violet said. "It looks like he left in a hurry. I wonder if—"

"He's probably on an errand," Jessie said.

They continued down the road, and Henry stopped suddenly. He pointed to the trail behind Mrs. Riley's house. A stooped figure was moving through the brush.

"Is that Daniel?" Benny asked.

"I don't think so," Jessie said. "That person is all hunched over."

"But what if he's about to change into the werewolf?" Benny said. "Can we follow him?"

Henry looked toward town. Streetlights had begun to blink on. "Okay," he said. "But we better hurry. It's getting dark."

5

A Pile of Bones

It was late afternoon as the Alden children climbed the trail behind Mrs. Riley's house. They kept Watch on his leash so he wouldn't scare any wildlife. When Watch stopped at a creek for a drink, Henry said, "Good idea, Watch. Let's take a break." He unzipped his pack for his water bottle. The others did the same.

"We need to stay hydrated like Watch, especially in this dry climate," Jessie said.

Violet laughed. "He would chase fish if we let him. See how he splashes right in?"

"Watch is smart all right," Benny boasted. "I bet he'll help us find clues up here."

Henry said, "Let's follow the creek up to that

ridge then turn around. We need to get back before dark." He picked up the pace. As they continued to hike through the sagebrush, they noticed footprints in the path.

"You can tell all sorts of people have been up here," Jessie observed. "This waffle pattern must be from a hiking boot."

"And over by the water. Aren't these prints from bare feet in the mud?" Violet asked.

"I think so," Henry said. "Someone must have gone wading."

Suddenly Benny hurried forward in the trail. He pointed to a set of paw prints. "Hey! A big dog was here. But, wait a minute. Where did it go?" Benny looked in every direction, but the prints had disappeared.

His sisters followed the path then stopped. "That's weird," said Jessie. "It looks like the dog just vanished. I don't know where it could have gone."

"The werewolf!" Benny cried. He held his finger in the air to explain his idea. "The human part had to take off his shoes before changing into the animal part. These big ol' paw prints are before he went back to being a human."

"Then where did he put his shoes?" Violet wanted to know. "They must be somewhere around here so he could wear them when he became human again."

Benny gazed at the trail then looked over at the creek. He shrugged. "I guess I don't know. But let's keep looking."

The children continued up the hill, past a wall of black lava. The trail switched back and forth as they climbed higher. At the ridge they rested to enjoy the view of Townsend. The tree-lined streets and the park resembled a miniature village. They could see the volleyball court and the barn. People sat on benches, watching children on the playground. Tiny flecks of light came from the picnic tables.

"Oh, they've lit up the jack-o'-lanterns," Jessie said. "They're pretty from up here."

Henry surveyed the scene then said, "People hiking up here have a good view. Someone could have been watching the barn."

"Waiting for it to get dark," Jessie said, finishing her brother's thought. "They would have known when to sneak in with the rake."

"And smash things up," Benny finished.

With worry in her voice, Violet said, "All those kids worked so hard on their jack-o'-lanterns. I hope no one wrecks them."

"Same here," said Henry. "Let's go a little farther while there's still a little light. We might find more clues to help Mrs. Riley."

As they went up the hill, Watch began tugging at his leash.

"What is it, boy?" Henry asked. "Where are we going?"

Watch pulled harder. He led the children off the trail through a cluster of juniper trees. Around a bend they came to a rocky clearing. It was high enough that the final minutes of sun lit the area.

"Oh gross," Violet cried. "Something died here."

Watch pulled Henry ahead to a patch of flat rock. The black stones were covered with bones and antlers. A man was crouching in the middle of the clearing. He was packing the bones into a burlap sack.

"Daniel?" Henry called from a distance.

But when the man turned to look at Henry, he

stepped back. It was not Daniel. The man had a full beard. His hair was dark and curly to his shoulders. His bare arms were covered with hair.

Watch barked just as Jessie, Violet, and Benny arrived. Startled, the man dropped the bag and ran through the woods.

"Who was that?" Henry said. "I feel bad that we scared him."

"Well, he scared me!" Violet said. "I've never seen anyone that furry except for a bear at the zoo. And what was he doing with all those bones?"

Once again, Benny had an idea. "How about this?" he said. "Maybe that hairy man is related to the werewolf. Maybe he was cleaning up after the wolf's last meal. They eat animals, don't they?"

Even though the bones didn't smell and there was no meat on them, Violet and Jessie backed away from the pile. "I'm not touching those things," Violet said.

"Me neither," her sister said. "I say we head back. It's almost sunset."

The western sky glowed orange and pink as the sun slipped behind the mountains. The air grew chilly. Without discussion the Aldens took out their sweatshirts. They drank sips of water. Then they dug in their packs for their flashlights. The trail downhill quickly grew dark. Henry led the way, and Jessie brought up the rear with Watch. She kept looking over her shoulder.

"I hope that hairy man doesn't come this way," she called to the others.

"I think he went in the other direction," Henry called back, slowing their pace. "Hey, everyone, be careful where you step. It's rocky." He looked over the edge. The trail narrowed as it twisted down the hill. Henry often glanced back at Violet and Benny to make sure they were okay. Their lights bounced against the growing shadows of dusk.

They reached the bottom of the hill as a light went on in Mrs. Riley's kitchen. They could see her through the window. She stood at the stove with Grandfather.

Benny yelled, "Hooray, I smell spaghetti! I'm starving."

"How was your day?" Grandfather asked when all were seated at the table.

The Legend of the Howling Werewolf

The children described the mysterious damage in the barn.

"They were a great help cleaning up," Mrs. Riley said.

"And then we got to make jack-o'-lanterns!" Benny said with excitement. "Mine is the one with a cowboy hat made out of leaves."

As Grandfather and Mrs. Riley discussed the weather, the children grew sleepy. They were tired from the long day and their big hike. When it came time to help with the dishes, they had forgotten to mention the hairy man and the pile of bones.

***

After dessert, Mrs. Riley brought in wood for the fireplace. "Sometimes it snows early in Idaho," she told the children. "Especially in these higher elevations. I want to make sure you're warm tonight."

Since this was their second evening in Townsend, the Alden children felt at home. The den was cozy with shelves of books, games, and magazines. A jigsaw puzzle was spread out on a card table. Soon the children unrolled their sleeping bags in front of the fireplace. The rising moon cast a glow through the blinds as they drifted to sleep.

A sudden howl from outside woke the children. Henry bolted up. Jessie and Violet grabbed each other's hand. Benny fumbled for his flashlight. They crept down the hall to the kitchen. As quietly as possible, they opened the back door and stepped outside. To their amazement, they saw a silhouette of someone staggering along the ridge. It had the head of a wolf. In the light of the rising moon, they could see its jaws opening with a howl.

In an excited whisper Benny said, "Just like the website! I knew it. There really is a werewolf!"

Violet rubbed her arms to keep warm, but more so because she was nervous.

Henry stared at the silhouette. "It sure looks like one," he said. "It's getting harder to believe they're not real."

"Now I'm wondering too," Jessie whispered.

Unanswered Questions

The next day after breakfast the children headed to town. It was a beautiful, crisp morning with an aroma of wood smoke from fireplaces filling the air. Frost on the rooftops sparkled in the sun. When they passed Daniel's cottage, he was in his garden. They waved to him, but Daniel only scowled. He hurried over to his chicken coop. Without looking at the Aldens, he rolled the cage to a sunny spot in the yard. Hens cackled and flurried as they pecked for worms in their new location.

"That's a really smart way to keep chickens safe," Violet said. "That way they won't get lost or run into the street. But why is Daniel ignoring us?"

"I hope he's okay," Jessie said.

"Maybe he's tired from the howling last night. It sure made me nervous," Violet said.

"I can't wait to tell him about the werewolf," Benny said.

Henry said, "Let's wait. We can say hi another time. It looks like he's busy."

At the park Mrs. Riley greeted the children by the picnic tables. "Good morning, children," she said. "I'm relieved to say there was no damage last night." She and Grandfather were pulling a protective blanket off the jack-o'-lanterns. The blanket was woven with bright stripes.

"That is such a beautiful blanket," Jessie said. "I've never seen one like it."

"It was handed down from my great-grandmother," Mrs. Riley said with pride. "Its thick wool kept away the moisture last night."

It was a bright day. The rope of colored flags fluttered in the breeze. "Everything looks so pretty," Violet said as she took out her camera. "I'll take some photos for my report. Cheese!" she yelled to her brothers. When Henry and Benny gave goofy smiles, Violet took their picture. She took one of Grandfather then several of Mrs. Riley unfolding her blanket. Finally she took one of Mrs. Riley and Jessie holding up the blanket. It was as tall as Grandfather.

Jessie took several pictures of the jack-o'-lanterns.

"When will the judging take place?" Henry asked.

"Tomorrow," Mrs. Riley replied. "I'm so please with all the creativity and fun designs."

"They certainly are imaginative," Grandfather said. "I admire how you used pointy pine cones for noses and leaves for hair. Well done. Say, how did you children sleep last night?"

"Just fine," Henry said.

"Well, not me," a woman interrupted. Her hair was messy, and she wore bedroom slippers. "That howling. Just like the website predicted." She handed Mrs. Riley her volunteer badge. "My kids heard the werewolf last night. They're too upset to participate today. I'm sorry, Susan."

A group of volunteers were in conversation as they walked from the parking lot. Two women handed Mrs. Riley their badges. One of them said,

Unanswered Questions

"The moon was rising. The howl scared the wits out of me. And it'll be a full harvest moon tomorrow."

"I showed my neighbor the website," another said. "Now he refuses to bring his kids."

A man in a grocer's apron approached. His name tag read, Mitch, Manager, Green Spot Organic Foods. "I realize this Harvest Festival is important," he said to Mrs. Riley. "But my customers are telling me it should be canceled. Who knows if there will be danger?"

"Mitch, you've been a big supporter of this event," Mrs. Riley said. "We'll be serving your fruits and veggies as appetizers for the evening picnic."

"I'm sorry, Susan," said Mitch. He threw up his hands and walked away.

Mrs. Riley stood tall, but the Alden children could see a slight slump to her shoulders. She seemed discouraged. "Please don't worry," she told the group. "Hysteria won't solve anything. I believe the legend of a howling werewolf is just that. A legend."

But the volunteers surrounding her in the park seemed nervous. They shifted uneasily on their feet. They looked toward the foothills. They whispered to one another. Hands in pockets, they shook their heads.

"If we hear howling again tonight," one of them told Mrs. Riley, "we will call Mayor Chang. We'll insist that she cancel all activities this weekend."

"We can't take any chances," another said. "Any kind of wild animal, wolf or whatever, running amok in town would be a disaster. What if it attacked a child?"

"That's right," an angry man said. "It probably has rabies."

Just then Ellen jogged through the park with her dog. When Kamu and Watch saw each other, they wagged their tails. They nuzzled each other. The two dogs were good friends now.

"Good morning, everyone," Ellen said to the volunteers. Several were her friends. They told her about the frightening events of last night.

"What?" Ellen asked. "This is the first I've heard of any werewolf." She patted Kamu's head then cast a worried look toward the foothills. She regarded the yellow flags by the volleyball court marking the fun run. "Are you sure?" she asked the group. "I always thought werewolves were from fairy tales. Like elves and giants. Right, kids?"

Violet said, "But we saw it last night."

"You're kidding," a teenage boy said. "You actually saw it?"

Benny excitedly described the late night, the rising moon, the strange shape, and the eerie howl.

Henry said, "Actually what we saw was a silhouette. It was weird. It looked exactly like the furry head of a big animal."

"Are you sure?" a teenage girl asked.

"I know what we saw," Benny insisted.

"It wasn't normal, that's for sure," Violet said.

A woman in sneakers and a ball cap walked briskly into the park. She wore a small backpack. She smiled at Mrs. Riley, and they waved to each other. "Oh, good," Mrs. Riley said. "Here comes Mayor Chang. She lives close by. She doesn't have a car, so she walks everywhere."

"I've heard people are upset," Mayor Chang said to the volunteers. "I don't think there's anything to worry about. We absolutely must have the festival."

Her backpack rustled with her lunch and with papers as she took out a clipboard.

A volunteer stood with his arms crossed. "Why is the festival so important?" he asked.

"The City Council and I have a big announcement," the mayor said. From her clipboard, she passed around some brochures. The pages showed photos of a white farmhouse with a red barn. Cattle grazed near a cornfield. A horse corral had a riding ring. "Good things are coming to Townsend," Mayor Chang said. "We'd like the whole town to be present when we explain. These pictures are examples of what can be built on the empty acres around here."

"And since this is our first Harvest Festival," Mrs. Riley said, "we want people to feel happy. It will give our community something to look forward to each year."

The Alden children and the volunteers listened. They studied the brochures. Finally one of one of the adults said, "All right. Let's wait and see what happens tonight."

But Henry spoke quietly to his sisters and brother. "I think I know why Daniel is upset," he said.

***

Grandfather brought a bag of burgers to the picnic table. Henry spread out some napkins. Benny opened little packs of ketchup and dumped a pile of French fries in the center of the table. Violet poked straws into the drink cups.

"I'm going to run some errands for Mrs. Riley," Grandfather told them. "Do you all have enough to keep you busy here?"

"Oh yes. We'll be fine, Grandfather," Jessie said. She took out her notebook. Clicking her pen a few times she said, "We need to solve a few things."

Grandfather smiled. "I'll leave you to it then. See you all at dinner. I'm going to be cooking my specialty."

"Do you mean veggie soup with your light, flaky, super-wonderful biscuits?' Violet asked. "With drops of honey and cinnamon?"

Grandfather's familiar grin answered for her. "You're right," he said. "Now all of you have fun this afternoon. I'm looking forward to seeing the full moon tonight."

"So are we," Benny said.

"Who knows what we'll discover when it rises over the foothills," Henry said. "See you later, Grandfather."

Though the air was cool, the warm sunshine made it pleasant. While eating lunch, the children discussed the werewolf. "I feel sorry for Mrs. Riley," Benny said. "She just wants to help her community. Now the whole town is too scared to come to the festival."

Jessie put her pen on her notebook. "Then we have to solve this mystery before the festival gets canceled. Where should we begin?" she asked.

"Let's start with the suspects," Henry said. He counted on his fingers. "First there's Daniel."

Jessie wrote, "Daniel, the conservationist."

"He seems nice," Benny said. "But he wasn't honest. He pretended Mrs. Riley told him about us and the sage grouse."

"So if Daniel didn't do anything," Henry said, "why did he lie?"

Violet sat up straight on the bench. She said, "That's what I wonder. Also, why was Daniel unfriendly when we went by his house this morning? He's busy, but he could have waved. Do you think he's uncomfortable seeing us?"

"Or is he embarrassed for being out late at night, chasing sage grouse?" Benny wondered.

"These are good questions," Jessie said. Head down, she wrote neatly in her notebook. "Next?"

"The strange guy with the beard and hairy arms," Henry said.

"He gave me the creeps!" said Violet. "What was he doing with all those bones? Yuck. And the antlers?"

"We definitely need to figure out more about

him," Jessie said as she wrote. She held up her pen. "Next?"

"Who smashed the pumpkins and sugar beets?" Violet asked.

"Right," Jessie said, writing across the page. "We definitely need to find that person. Next?"

Benny said, "Add Ellen's dog, Kamu. He's big enough to be a werewolf. At least I think he is. Or maybe a werewolf's best friend."

"I've never heard any legends of a dog becoming a werewolf," Henry said, chuckling. "Or being friends with one."

"You are right that Kamu has a mysterious background, Benny," Jessie said. "Since he was a rescue, no one knows why he's so afraid of getting his paws wet."

"Are werewolves afraid of water?" Benny asked.

Henry smiled. "You're thinking of the Toothless Trolls, Benny. Another legend," he said. "They melt if they fall in a river."

Violet looked under the picnic table. Watch slept peacefully by their feet. She said, "Watch would play in a creek all day if we let him. He's not afraid."

Unanswered Questions

"We need some more clues in a hurry," Jessie said. She snapped her notebook shut and returned it to her pack. "Let's look around."

Not Normal Footprints

When the Alden children finished their burgers and fries, they took their paper trash to the recycling. They put their lids, straws, and ketchup packets in the plastics bin. As they looked around, they realized they were alone in the park. Mrs. Riley wasn't anywhere to be seen. Grandfather had driven to town. On this beautiful autumn day, there were suddenly no families in the picnic area. No children played on the jungle gym or swings. The volleyball court was empty. Only two teenage girls on rollerblades broke the silence. The girls swooped around the empty parking lot then skated away.

"Where is everyone?" Benny asked.

"That's what I wonder," Violet said. She twisted one of her pigtails around her finger, as if she was nervous.

"This is bizarre," Henry said. He went to the sign that said Harvest Festival This Weekend. Everyone Welcome. It was ripped in half and dangling in the dirt.

"Hey! I bet the werewolf did this," Benny said.

"Or," Jessie said, "it was someone protesting the event."

"Well, however it happened," Henry said, "it's not good. This is our third day in Townsend, and the festival is tomorrow. We have to get to the bottom of things. And fast."

"I agree," Jessie said.

The Aldens looked at one another with questions.

"Maybe Mrs. Riley is in the barn," Henry said. "Let's see if there's anything we can do for her."

Benny and Watch led the way. The barn was cool inside. All the hay had been neatly swept into the horse stalls. There was no further damage to the large crates of pumpkins and sugar beets. "Hello?" Jessie called. "Mrs. Riley?"

Mrs. Riley's office in the back of the barn had a Dutch door. The children peered in over the top and looked around. Her woven blanket was folded on a shelf. Photos of horses with blue award ribbons hung on the rough wooden walls. A framed university diploma identified Susan Dawn Riley as a professor of Native American arts.

"Oh wow," Jessie said. "Mrs. Riley is very modest about her accomplishments."

Violet noticed some photos showing Mrs. Riley with the mayor and business leaders. "It looks like she has been very involved in Townsend for a long time. I can see why this event is so important to her."

"All the more reason to solve this mystery," Henry said. "Let's head back to the foothills. We might find the spot where we saw that silhouette last night. There are bound to be prints from whatever that thing was, don't you think?"

"Yes!" Benny cried. "I'm ready. Let's go exploring."

The children hurried from the barn. They walked through the park then down Main Street. When they rounded the corner they could see Daniel by his back fence, pruning a rosebush. Once again, he kept his eyes down as the Aldens passed his house. Farther down the road, Benny said, "I still wonder why Daniel isn't friendly to us."

"Maybe he's busy and embarrassed," said Jessie. "If I got caught in a lie I would have a hard time being social too."

They continued to Mrs. Riley's house. Her car wasn't in her driveway. Grandfather's car was also gone. Henry said, "No one's home yet, so we have plenty of time to investigate."

In the kitchen the children refilled their water bottles. Jessie tore a sheet of paper from her notebook. "Dear Grandfather and Mrs. Riley," she wrote. "We are on a short hike. Watch is with us, so don't worry. We'll be back in time to help with dinner." She signed her name then handed her pen to Henry. He signed then so did Violet. Benny drew a cat with a smiley face. Then in neat block letters he printed, LOVE, BENNY. They set the message by the bowl of fruit.

On the way up the twisty trail, the Aldens spotted a runner ahead of them with a big dog beside them.

The Legend of the Howling Werewolf

The runner had stopped on the path. She held two poles with yellow flags.

"Oh, it's Ellen," Violet said. "And Kamu. Hi, Ellen!"

"Hello there," the woman said. She pushed her sunglasses to the top of her head. "Nice to see you all again. I'm marking the starting line for the fun run. It begins tomorrow at noon."

"Where will everyone go from here?" Benny asked.

With a grunt, Ellen planted the poles on either side of the trail. She pointed up hill. "That way," she said. "Runners will head to the ridge then down the far slope. They'll circle the duck pond and the community garden on their way down to the park. The finish line is by the volleyball court. In all, it is about three miles."

"Three miles, whew! That's a long way," Jessie said.

"Are you all walking the course this afternoon?" Ellen asked. She gave them a friendly smile. "I'm serious. You kids look strong. You could make it, I'm sure."

Not Normal Footprints

"Not today," Henry said. "We're just going up a bit farther. At the ridge, we'll turn around and come back this way. Our grandfather would worry if we went on a long hike without telling him."

Ellen said, "I understand. See you in a little bit. I'll still be here. Kamu's paws are sore from stepping in that awful cheat grass. I removed the thorns, but I think he needs to rest for a while. We could sit here all day. The view of the town and the park is so beautiful."

The Aldens continued up hill. Once again, Watch led them off the trail to where they had been yesterday. Out of breath from the climb, the children rested for a moment among the trees. The clearing resembled a low table of black stone, pocked by tiny holes. The edges were rounded where they had flowed onto the cooler earth thousands of years earlier.

"Look at this lava," said Henry. "I didn't notice it yesterday because of all the stuff covering it."

"I can't believe there are old volcanoes around here," Benny said. "I wish we could go up close to one and look down inside."

"Maybe some day, Benny," said his brother.

"This will be great for my report," Violet said. "We're also studying geology." She took out her camera to document their surroundings.

As they looked around, they noticed something different. The bones were gone. The antlers were gone. Skinny lines in the sand looked as if someone had swept the area clean.

"What happened here?" Henry asked.

"This feels weird," Jessie said.

Benny went over to one of the juniper pines. Leaning against its trunk was a broken limb. He picked up the branch and pulled it through the dirt. Its pine needles acted as a broom. And these pine needles matched the skinny lines in the clearing.

"I think someone took the bones," he said, "then swept up all the little pieces with this."

"Why would they do that?" Jessie asked.

"Good question," her older brother responded. "Let's keep following the creek and go up a bit farther."

***

From the ridge, the Aldens could see Mrs. Riley's

house. Henry pointed downhill and said, "There's the spot outside where we were standing last night. Ha! If someone was up here looking down, I bet Mrs. Riley's light made us look like silhouettes."

"That's funny!" Jessie said. "Maybe two shadows staring at each other. Anyway, back to business. I bet if we search around we'll find foot or paw prints from whoever was up here." She stepped carefully on a patch of ground that was moist from the creek. A single set of prints squished the mud.

Benny bent down to take a look. "These look like they were made by bare feet. Human bare feet," he said. "I was hoping to find some big werewolf prints!"

Jessie also bent down to look. "These aren't from a normal human. Check out this little mark in the center of each footprint."

"Four dots inside a circle?" Henry said. "Each footprint has the same one. Hmm. I've seen these somewhere." He squinted as he tried to remember.

Jessie said, "So have I. It's some kind of logo."

"What's a logo?" Benny asked.

"It's a special symbol used to identify things," Jessie answered.

Benny thought a moment. "You mean like the street signs? They all show a sage hen."

"That's right, Benny," Jessie said. "The sage hen

is a logo for Townsend."

"So then the potato is kind of a logo for Idaho?" he added.

"Makes sense to me," said his brother. "But what kind of person has a logo on the bottom of their feet?"

"Whoa," Violet gasped. "Wait a second." Her camera was still around her neck. She scrolled through the digital photos. "Look at these."

Benny and Violet looked, then Henry and Jessie did as well. They took turns cupping the screen to block the sun's glare.

Jessie laughed. "Good work, Violet. I think we know where our next stop should be."

Close Encounter

Grinning from their discovery, the Alden children returned to the trail. Ellen was still sitting in the sunshine looking out over the town and the park. Kamu slept at her side.

"Hi, Miss Ellen!" Violet called. "We found something to show you."

"Really? What is it?" she asked.

Benny, too, was excited. "The mysterious footprints!" he cried. "We solved the werewolf mystery. Well, at least part of it."

"But we still have some questions," Jessie added.

Ellen stood up then brushed off her leggings. "I'm curious what you mean," she said.

Violet showed her the digital photos. They were

from the Aldens' first day in the park when the children had met her. Violet tapped the screen. With her finger and thumb, she pinched an image to enlarge it. It showed Ellen leaping like a dancer and showed the bottom of her toe shoes.

"I'm not sure what your point is," said Ellen.

Violet tapped again, to further enlarge the square with four dots. "We found this marking up the path. It was in the mud," she explained. She showed Ellen photos of the mud prints.

Jessie said, "The logo made us realize the prints weren't from bare feet."

"Oh, is this what you mean?" Ellen asked. "I bought these special shoes from the Swim and Run Shop in Townsend." She balanced on one leg and turned her foot. The bottoms of her toe shoes were muddy, but the children could see the logo.

"We've been thinking," Henry said. "At first we wondered if a werewolf might make these prints after changing into a human. That is if werewolves are even real."

"Which we don't believe they are," Jessie said. "Now it seems someone has been impersonating the werewolf. And we think that person is you."

"Oh dear," Ellen said. "I was worried this was going to happen. I guess I should come clean." She looked out over the quiet town then back at the children. "I go on night runs in the foothills when no one's around. As the moon becomes full, it's so bright I don't even need a headlamp. I can see way out over the desert and to the Rocky Mountains. It's beautiful. Beautiful and peaceful."

"But aren't you afraid being out here alone?" Violet asked.

"I feel safe jogging with Kamu," Ellen said. "Even though he is a wimp about getting his feet wet, I'm sure he will protect me."

Jessie thought a moment. "Have you been running at night for very long?"

"Since June," Ellen answered. "Summer days are so hot in Idaho, I wait till sundown to hit the trails."

Henry turned to his family. "When did Mrs. Riley say the werewolf rumor started?"

"A couple months ago," Jessie said. "When she put up the website and started planning the

Harvest Festival."

"That's what I thought," said Henry. "Miss Ellen, on your night runs, what happens when Kamu comes to the creek up here?"

"He starts crying," Ellen replied. "Even a trickle of water bothers his feet. He'll refuse to jump over it, so in the muddy spots I have to lift him."

The children stared at Ellen in wonder. "Could you please show us how you do that?" Jessie asked.

Ellen patted her chest. "Here, Kamu. Here, boy." The malamute uncurled from his nap and stretched. Ellen continued to pat her chest until he stood on his hind legs.

"Like this," she demonstrated. She bent her knees to hug his torso. With an "ooooph" she lifted him then staggered a few paces. Kamu hung on her back like a furry cape. His furry head nearly covered her face. When he began to squirm, she leaned forward to gently let him down. "He's really heavy," she said. "But I only carry him past the puddles. It's the only way he'll keep going."

"Does he cry at night when you lift him?" Henry asked.

"Oh yes. First he whimpers, then he howls. Big dogs like malamutes don't like the feeling of being carried by a human. It throws off their balance. It definitely scared Kamu, but he's more afraid of getting his feet wet."

"Now I get it," Jessie said. "So that's what we saw from Mrs. Riley's yard. We were seeing you carrying Kamu on your back."

"Aha!" Benny cried. "You and Kamu are the werewolf!"

"I'm very sorry I scared so many people," Ellen said. "The other day in the park I was stunned to hear the rumor. I went home and looked at the website. Someone had posted photos of the foothills just as the moon was rising. I admit the silhouette looked like a giant wolf standing on its hind legs."

"Then since you weren't trying to fool anyone, why didn't you say anything?" Henry asked. "Mrs. Riley is worried and upset."

"I'm sorry," Ellen said again. "I was embarrassed. I'm not supposed to be running on the trail at night. It's been closed for safety."

Close Encounter

Henry glanced up the hill then down. "But is it safe now?" he asked.

"It is," said Ellen. "The other night I filled in a few gopher holes, which were actually made by those little mousy creatures called voles. And I cleared away some large rocks that had tumbled into the path. We're all set for tomorrow's run. I just hope people will still show up."

As they stood in the afternoon sun, the dogs were panting from the heat. Jessie took a collapsible bowl from her backpack then poured in some water. Watch and Kamu were thirsty. They drank and drank. When they had slurped the bowl dry, Jessie raised her hand as a signal to sit. Watch obeyed. Next she tapped her hip pocket. He raised his front paw to shake her hand.

"Good boy, Watch," Jessie said as she gave him a biscuit. Kamu cocked his head in curiosity. Now he sat. He lifted his paw to shake. "Yes!" Jessie cried. She rewarded him with a treat then turned to Ellen.

"Look how smart Kamu is," Jessie said. "See how fast he copied Watch? I bet you could train him to not be afraid of water."

Ellen laughed. She bent down to pet both dogs. She hugged Kamu then kissed his furry head. "You might be right, Jessie," she said. "That would be so wonderful."

Benny put his hands in his pockets. He rocked on his heels. "I still wonder about something, Miss Ellen. Did you take away all the bones?"

"What bones?" she said.

The children explained what they had seen the day before. They described the hairy man. "Now the bones aren't there any more," Violet said.

"Hmm, that's odd," said Ellen. "I didn't go that way, kids. I stayed on the main path. And I don't know anyone in town who fits that description. Sounds like strange behavior."

***

The children and Ellen walked down the hill together. Watch and Kamu wandered ahead, exploring the sagebrush. The dogs wagged and sniffed and crisscrossed the trail.

"Good-bye," said Ellen. "See you later. Tomorrow's the big day."

Back at the house Grandfather was in the

kitchen with Mrs. Riley. The oven was heating. He was rolling dough for his flaky biscuits while she chopped onions.

While the children described their afternoon, Jessie read aloud the clues in her notebook. She put question marks by "Hairy Man" and "Unfriendly Daniel." She checked off "Silhouette" and "Odd Footprints."

"We think people saw Ellen carrying Kamu over her shoulder," Henry explained.

"The howling was Kamu too," Violet added.

"Because he was scared!" Benny finished.

Mrs. Riley smiled at the Alden children. Her brown eyes gleamed. "This is a huge relief," she said. "I knew the werewolf was just a legend, but I'm still puzzled. Who is spreading the rumors? And why?"

"We need to stop that person," Violet said. "Otherwise no one will show up to the festival!"

"May we check the website?" Jessie asked Mrs. Riley. "We might find more clues."

"Please do," Mrs. Riley said.

Jessie logged on to the Harvest Festival website.

"Oh no," she whispered.

"What?" the others asked.

"A new post was added this morning," Jessie said. She read aloud. "'Close Encounter! Listen to the werewolf growl and scare away these sage grouse. Click here.'" A link showed a video. The camera followed three sage grouse waddling into a thicket of sagebrush. There was a sudden growling of a dog from the other side of the thicket. Suddenly the birds flew up in a noisy rush, and the camera cut off.

Close Encounter

The Aldens looked at one another. They looked at Grandfather, then at Mrs. Riley. Finally Henry said, "Aren't those the birds we saw our first night here?"

"And that was Watch growling!" Benny cried. "Watch, you're a werewolf!"

Watch perked his head up at the sound of his name. Then he put it back down and wagged his tail.

Jessie tapped her pen on the table, thinking. "We know of one other person out that night."

"Who?" Mrs. Riley asked.

"Yes, who?" Grandfather asked.

Violet said, "Daniel. Daniel the conservationist!"

CHAPTER 9

Pumpkin Guts

A large pot of soup simmered on the stove as the Aldens and Mrs. Riley sat around the kitchen table. The children told about their midnight walk in the foothills. They described meeting Daniel the next morning.

Mrs. Riley shook her head sadly. "I'm so disappointed," she said. "Daniel has been a good neighbor for years. He and I like to barter. I bring him homemade bread, and he gives me a dozen fresh eggs. We like to practice some of the old-time ways. That's how people used to get by. They traded things they needed or they helped with chores."

Mrs. Riley sat quietly with her thoughts.

After a moment Henry glanced out the window.

"It's still light out, Mrs. Riley. Maybe we could go talk to Daniel. I'm sure he has an explanation."

"Tomorrow's the big day," Violet reminded everyone.

"So maybe it's not too late to save the festival," Jessie said.

Benny rubbed his stomach. "I'm hungry. But Grandfather's soup tastes even better the longer it cooks. And we can bake the biscuits later. I want to hear what Daniel says."

"You mean now?" Mrs. Riley asked. Her smile was broad. "I like your ideas, children. Okay, we'll eat later. Is that okay, James?"

Grandfather nodded. He turned the stove to low then spread aluminum foil over the biscuit dough. He put on his wool sweater.

"Here's a snack to hold us over," Mrs. Riley said. She passed around a bowl of apples. Then she grabbed her down vest from a hook by the back door. "Button up, everyone. It's chilly out."

***

Daniel was closing up his chicken coop. He clicked on a warm light in the pen. Then he went to his wheelbarrow. "Might freeze tonight," he told his visitors. He wore a "Save the Sage Grouse" T-shirt under his jacket. From his pocket he took out his black knit cap. It matched his hair, but instead of putting it on, he wrung it between his hands. "But I guess you're not here to talk about the weather."

"Not exactly," Mrs. Riley said. Her face was stern. She gestured toward her friends. "Daniel, I understand you've already met my weekend guests, the Alden family."

"Yes, I have. Good evening, Mr. Alden," Daniel said in a quiet voice. "Hello, kids."

"You told these children something that wasn't true," said Mrs. Riley. "I want you to make things right."

The group stood awkwardly. Their breaths made frost in the cold air. Grandfather looked at his grandchildren. He could see they were bursting with questions. With a nod he smiled at them, urging them to speak.

"Daniel?" Benny began. "Why did you lie to us?"

"Why were you really out the other night?" said Jessie.

The Legend of the Howling Werewolf

"And why did you pretend our dog was the growling werewolf?" Henry said. "You've scared a lot of people for no good reason."

Daniel took a deep breath. "Okay," he said. "Here's what happened. A few weeks ago, I posted a werewolf rumor on the website. Some folks in town are superstitious, so I knew they would freak out. And I knew they would spread the story."

Mrs. Riley shook her head. Her jaw was tight.

Daniel avoided her angry look and continued. "Then the other night when I was following the sage grouse, I saw you kids in the foothills. With my phone I took a video. Your dog barking was a bonus. I thought adding it to the website would make the rumor more believable."

"That's dishonest," Jessie said.

"And why make up a story in the first place?" Henry asked.

"I'm embarrassed to say I wanted to scare people," Daniel said.

"Well it sure worked," Benny said. "And now everyone's upset."

Mrs. Riley opened her hands in a question. "I

don't understand. You and I are friends, Daniel. You know how important this first Harvest Festival is to our community."

"I do know that," Daniel said. "I went about it all wrong. I'm truly sorry."

"I'm more sad than angry," Mrs. Riley said. "What's really going on here?"

"There's no excusing what I did," Daniel replied. He put on his hat then blew on his hands to keep them warm. "Mayor Chang and the city council have a big announcement tomorrow. I'm worried sick about it. Have you seen the fancy brochures she's been passing out on her walks through town?"

"Yes, of course I have. I'm on the city council too," Mrs. Riley said.

"Well, Townsend leaders want to devote more land to farming," Daniel explained to Grandfather Alden. "I think they should reconsider. Bulldozers and tractors will have a terrible effect on the sage grouse. Tourists love to come to see these birds. Our town benefits from the money they spend here. Motels, meals, and snacks." Daniel opened his jacket to show his T-shirt. "And they always buy souvenirs."

Mrs. Riley thought a moment. "You're right," she said. "But you're a smart man, Daniel. Didn't you try to communicate with anyone?"

"Oh yes, quite a lot. But the mayor didn't respond to my emails. When I called her, she was either in a meeting or out walking around. I felt like no one cared."

The children listened. Mrs. Riley and Grandfather listened.

"I'm ashamed of my actions," Daniel said. "I owe an apology to you children. And especially to you, Susan. I should have come to you first. You and I have always been able to talk."

"We're talking now, Daniel, so do something. We can't waste another minute. The Harvest Festival is tomorrow," Mrs. Riley said. "We've planned a pancake breakfast. A fun run. A jack-o'-lantern contest and games. A dog parade with a marching band. Then a big picnic with fireworks after dark."

"I'm going online right now," Daniel said, hurrying for his front porch. "I'll straighten everything out. I promise."

***

"Well, guess I'll head on home," Mrs. Riley said. "I have phone calls to make, emails to send. Dinner's not for another hour, so take your time."

Grandfather said, "I'll come with you, Susan. I have some of my own emails to answer."

"The neighborhoods are safe if you kids want to explore a little," she said. "Everyone around here looks out for one another. You know how to find my street. The rising moon will light your way. Have fun."

The children kept Watch on his leash as they wandered the quiet streets. Cottages looked cozy with their windows lit as families settled in for the evening. Porch lights came on. It was getting cold.

Benny said, "I still have a big question."

"What is it, Benny?" Jessie asked.

"Who smashed up all that stuff in the barn?" he said. "That's part of the mystery too."

"Oh, you're right. One last clue," said Violet.

"When we were there the other day, we figured out it was someone with a rake," Jessie said. "We found one there. It made marks that looked like claws. So we know what caused it, but not who did it."

"Oh, hey!" Henry cried. "I just remembered something. Follow me." He walked briskly to the corner then turned down a dirt alley.

"Where are we going?" Violet asked.

"I think this is where I saw it," Henry said. "We wandered by here the other day on our way to town."

In the middle of the block they came to a back yard. Yellowed cornstalks lined the fence. There were two compost barrels inside. A stone path led to a tool shed. "There it is," Henry said, pointing.

"What are we looking for?" Benny asked.

Henry went to a cluster of tools leaning against a shed. There was a broom and mop, shovels, a hoe and ladder, and two rakes. He untangled one of the rakes and pulled it out. "I noticed this the other day and just now made the connection," he said.

The rake's tines were covered with pumpkin guts. A familiar chicken coop was in the center of the lawn.

"Wait a minute!" Benny cried. He looked around then hurried up the side yard. "Daniel lives here. This is his house. We're back where we started."

"Then let's knock on his door," Jessie said.

The children went onto the front porch. Through the window they could see a cozy room. There was a woodstove and a pleasant clutter of books. A cat slept in a wingback chair. Daniel sat on a small couch with his laptop, typing away. At first he didn't hear the children knock.

They tried again.

"Come in!" he finally answered.

Henry left the rake on the porch. "We're sorry to bother you, Daniel," he said. "We just have one more question. Benny?"

Benny asked about the barn.

Daniel went to the chair and picked up his cat. He held it in his arms. It purred loudly as he pet it. "Yes," he said. "I snuck into the barn with my rake. I also used the one there to make the claw marks."

The children watched Daniel. At that moment, it seemed his cat was his only friend in the world.

"But why make such a big sloppy mess?" Violet finally asked.

"I was trying to interrupt things," said Daniel. "I was wrong to let my frustrations get out of control. But before you kids go, let me show you something." He set his cat in the chair and returned to his laptop.

Daniel scrolled to the Harvest Festival website. He clicked through the comments and photos. "See? I deleted all the negative posts and the rumors. I'm about to write a public apology."

The children said good night then left Daniel's cottage. "We won't know until tomorrow if Daniel saved the festival," Henry said.

As they walked back to Mrs. Riley's the foothills glowed with moonlight. It was a beautiful, frosty night. They quickened their pace to stay warm, and because they were hungry.

"Dinner's going to taste better than ever tonight," said Benny.

"That's what you always say, Benny," Jessie said, chuckling. "But I think you might be right this time."

CHAPTER

10

A Big Announcement

After sunrise the next morning, the children walked to town, excited to get to the festival grounds. Jessie kept Watch on a leash so he wouldn't chase any cats. As they passed Daniel's garden, they waved to him. He was gathering eggs from his chicken coop. "See you at the festival," he called. "I'll have a surprise for you."

"I wonder what kind of surprise," Violet said.

Jessie glanced back at the cottage. "Daniel already told us he's sorry," she said. "He doesn't have to give us anything."

When the Aldens reached the park, they heard the happy chatter of children on the playground. Families were lining up for the breakfast cooking

99

on portable stoves. There was a good aroma of pancakes and sausage.

"I love pancakes!" Benny announced as he got his plate and stood in line.

"We know," Henry said with a laugh. "I'm just glad people are showing up. This is a good sign."

Long tables were decorated with jack-o'-lanterns. A man and woman with *Judge* badges were discussing the artistic sugar beets. They tacked award ribbons to each one. "Oh, look," Violet said. "Mine got Most Friendly. I like that. Where's yours, Benny?"

"Over there somewhere," he said. "Let's eat first then go looking around."

At the tables families passed jugs of maple syrup. They passed plates of butter and bowls of baked apples. Mrs. Riley came around with the pitcher of orange juice. "Good morning, all," she said. "Thank you for coming to our first Harvest Festival." A beautiful beaded clip held her dark hair away from her face. She looked happy and relaxed.

While the Alden children ate breakfast, they saw Daniel and Mayor Chang. The two stood by the large coffee jug with their insulated mugs from home. They were talking to each other. Daniel appeared to be listening to the mayor. Then she appeared to be listening to him. They refilled their mugs.

"I wonder what they're talking about," Violet said. "They seem to be having a serious conversation."

"At least they don't look mad," Benny said.

Just then the mayor reached out to shake Daniel's hand. They smiled at each other. They got more coffee then went to talk to other people.

"Whew," Henry said. "Looks like everything's okay."

"I'm relieved," Jessie said, "but we still have another question." She opened her notebook, and Henry read the clues. All but two were checked off.

"Oh, that's right," Henry said. "What happened to the bones we saw in the clearing?"

"And who was that hairy man?" Benny added.

"He sure acted like he was hiding something," said Violet.

Jessie returned her notebook to her pack. "I hope we can solve this mystery by tonight, before we leave tomorrow morning."

***

It was a sunny, cool day. The park was festive with flags and banners. Bunches of colored balloons bobbed in the breeze. The grassy field was busy with artists selling their goods. Their booths displayed paintings, homemade jams, and cookies. There were knit scarves and hats, quilts, and jewelry. Do your Christmas Shopping Early, read one sign. Another said From Creatures Big and Small. Follow the Arrows.

"What kind of creatures?" Benny wondered.

"Let's find out," said Violet.

The children wandered among the cheerful exhibits and tables. The arrows led to a three-sided tent with a wooden sign that said Idaho Originals—From Creatures Big and Small. Two tables displayed lamps and hat racks made from antlers. A chandelier hung from a tall pole. It had been wired together from a cluster of antlers with pointed tips. There were small toy animals carved from bone, also tiny flutes and whistles.

"Check out this coat rack," said Jessie. "It's identical to Mrs. Riley's, the one by her back door."

A Big Announcement

"Cool," said Benny.

"Wouldn't Grandfather like these?" Henry said. He was admiring a set of checkers. The white markers were from bones. The black ones had tiny holes in their surfaces. "Are these from lava?" he asked the man behind the table.

"That's right," he answered. "Years ago it flowed from active volcanoes around here. The desert is full of lava fields." The man had a full beard that lifted when he smiled at the Aldens. His eyes twinkled as if he knew them. But Benny just stared at him. Jessie and Violet gasped. Henry caught his breath and said, "We saw you in the foothills the other day! You were putting bones and stuff into a big bag."

"Oh, was that you children? I have to admit it was a rather odd way to meet," he said. The bearded man wore a long-sleeved flannel shirt and a down vest to protect against the autumn chill. His long curly hair was pulled back into a ponytail. "My name's Cal. What are yours?"

The children introduced themselves. They described their weekend and the werewolf. "But

we couldn't figure out what all those bones were from," Henry told him.

"It seems we keep having more and more questions," Jessie said.

"Such as, what was I doing up there?" Cal asked with a smile.

"And what do bones have to do with the Harvest Festival?" Violet wanted to know.

"Those are very good questions," Cal said. He looked impressed. "I'm a different type of harvester. I go hiking through the woods and sagebrush. When deer shed their antlers on the ground, I gather them up. As for bones, when animals die in the wild, scavengers feast on their meat. Magpies and wolves are common around here, so I just wait for them to do their job. Then I collect the bones."

"That's a lot of work," Henry said. "What do you do then?"

"I soak them in a cleaning solution," Cal explained. "After they're sterilized, I spread them on a patch of lava. The black rock absorbs the heat and helps the drying process. Summer and early fall are best because of how these hillsides bake in the sun."

"How do you think of things to make?" Benny asked.

Cal smiled. "That is the best part. I haul everything home and imagine what I might create. It's peaceful and fun. I make my living by selling online and to neighbors. That's why I hurried away the other day. I'm not supposed to be using public land for my business, but laws are changing. I hope to get a permit soon."

"We're sorry we scared you," said Violet.

Cal laughed. "I'm sorry I scared you!"

***

Late that afternoon, smoke rose from a fire pit in the park. People arrived with picnic baskets and blankets to spread in the grass. Women from the Shoshone-Bannock tribe set up camp stoves to share Indian fry bread. Ellen brought a bucket of homemade ice cream to share.

Mayor Chang looked at the families settling in with their dinners. "I'm happy to see so many of you," she said. Her voice carried clearly through the brisk air. "As some of you know, we were going to have a big announcement today. But we have decided to wait."

A rustle went through the crowd.

"We'll have a town hall meeting next week," Mayor Chang continued. "It will be a chance for everyone to voice their opinions. Before we invite more development to our community, I've decided that all sides should be heard. It's wise to consider Idaho's wildlife and to think about the peaceful environment so dear to all of us."

Applause broke out. Someone shouted, "Terrific!" Another person yelled, "Thank you, Mayor Chang."

She gave a slight nod then held up her hand. "One last thing," she said. "I want to thank the Alden kids for helping us all put the silly rumors that have been floating around to rest. The Harvest Festival tradition may not have started at all without them. Have a wonderful evening, everyone."

***

Grandfather spread a quilt in the grass. Mrs. Riley opened a large wicker basket. She took out sandwiches and grapes. She said, "I've invited Daniel to join us. He has an award for each of you."

"An award? Really?" Jessie said.

"What for?" Henry asked.

Daniel soon arrived with a small canvas bag. "Good evening," he said. "Susan, may I present these before we eat? I see some wiggling."

Benny was so excited, he was sitting on his hands. His eyes were bright.

"By all means," Mrs. Riley said.

"So now the surprise," Daniel said to the children. "Several months ago my friends and I started a recycling program in Townsend. This weekend we noticed you kids picking up random papers and garbage. No one asked you to do this. And you've been sorting them into the proper bins. We're impressed."

Benny said, "Grandfather taught us to pick up after ourselves."

"But we don't need an award," said Jessie. "It's a habit."

"Well, anyway," Daniel continued, "I wanted to give you something to remember Townsend by. Something to carry home with you. It won't crumble like cookies or break like an egg." He opened his bag and took out four T-shirts. "Your grandfather told me your sizes."

"Yay!" Benny shouted. "I love cookies, but I like this too!"

"What does it say?" Violet asked.

"Save the Sage Grouse," said Jessie. "It's perfect. Thank you, Daniel."

Daniel smiled. "You kids are most welcome. We hope you come back to Townsend soon."

"I agree," said Mrs. Riley.

Benny was still excited. "Grandfather, can we please come back?" he said. "Maybe we could look for Bigfoot!"

Turn the page to read
a sneak preview of

THE DAY OF THE
DEAD MYSTERY

the next
Boxcar Children mystery!

When the Aldens arrived at the Hidalgos' the next morning, Gloria and Mrs. Hidalgo were just finishing setting up the materials for making the Day of the Dead decorations on the long table in the dining room.

"You look like yourself again," Violet said to Gloria. Now that Halloween was over, Gloria's dark, wavy hair hung down her back, and she had on her favorite gold earrings, shaped like tiny birds.

"I'll let you kids get to work," Mrs. Hidalgo said. She opened the door that revealed stairs down to the basement. "I'll be down in my studio if you need me."

"Are you working on something new?" Henry asked. Mrs. Hidalgo was an artist known for her colorful clay sculptures of animals. Back in September, Grandfather had taken the children to see a collection of her work at the Greenfield

Art Gallery.

"Yes," she said, "an iguana!" She wiggled her fingers the way iguanas moved their long, green toes. "But don't tell Mateo. I am going to give it to him for his birthday."

Benny gave her a serious nod. "We promise to keep it a secret."

Mrs. Hidalgo waved and disappeared down the stairs. Jessie looked at Gloria. "Where *is* Mateo?" Jessie asked. "Is he feeling better after eating all that Halloween candy?"

Gloria's smile faded. "Well, the good news is that he's feeling better. He was up early this morning and went out to see a friend. But I wish he were here to help make the decorations. He's usually so excited for Day of the Dead."

"Don't worry," Jessie said. "I'm sure he'll be back soon. And for now we're here to help."

"It's going to be fun," Gloria said, cheering up. She unwrapped a package of tissue paper that included every color of the rainbow.

Violet felt her imagination start to leap and dance as she imagined all the things they could make. "Where should we begin?" she asked Gloria.

"How about by cutting some paper?" said Gloria. "In Spanish this is called *papel picado*."

She picked up a piece of orange tissue paper from the top of the pile and showed the Aldens how to fold it and use the tip of a pair of scissors to cut out shapes. When she unfolded the paper again, light shone through the holes. "We will string all these together in a line and hang them from tree to tree in the park," she said. "When the breeze blows through them, they flutter in the air. I love the way they look."

"Oh, they must be so festive with all the different colors," Violet said. Benny selected a yellow piece of tissue and Violet chose pink. They both got to work cutting out the designs.

"This reminds me of cutting paper snowflakes with Mrs. McGregor when we had a snow day last winter," Benny said. "Remember how many we made?"

Jessie laughed. "We taped so many on the windows, Grandfather could hardly see inside when he came home."

"And poor Watch could hardly see *outside* to watch the squirrels," Benny said.

At the other end of the table, Gloria tore a piece of wax paper from a roll and spread it on a cookie sheet. Then she took the lid off a plastic food container and began carefully lifting out small white candies.

"Jessie, could you help me with the sugar skulls?" Gloria asked.

"Sure," Jessie said. She came down to Gloria's side of the table. "What are these for?"

"They are sugar skulls, or *calaveras de azúcar*. My mom did the first part by making the candies in the shape of skulls and setting them out to dry. Now we need to decorate them with frosting—the brighter and more creative, the better," she said.

"Did I hear someone say frosting?" Benny asked, perking up.

Gloria laughed. "We have a lot of decorating to do, so there's plenty of work to go around," she said. "Although most of these will go on the altar. The rest we can eat, but not until tomorrow."

"Hmm," Benny said. He was much more

interested in the eating than the decorating. "I think I'd better stick to paper."

Jessie laughed. "That's okay, Benny." She turned back to Gloria. "How do the skulls fit in to the celebration?" she asked. Skulls had always seemed spooky to her, but she could tell they meant something different to Gloria and her family.

"In our culture," Gloria said, "death isn't something to be afraid of. It's just a natural part of life. Bright colors and silly frosting faces painted on the skulls, plus music and games and good food, all help us remember to celebrate the people we lost instead of being sad."

Gloria helped Jessie spoon red, yellow, and purple frosting into separate pastry bags. Then she began to pipe designs on the sugar skulls and place them one by one on the cookie sheet to dry.

"Last but not least, we have the flowers," Gloria said. Henry said he would help with those. Gloria opened a new package of orange tissue paper and showed Henry how to fold a stack of sheets in an accordion pattern, tie them at the center, and fluff out the layers of paper until it looked like a marigold blossom.

"My mom will add these to the altar along with real marigold petals. The tradition says that the bright orange color and the beautiful scent of the flowers help guide spirits back to earth on this special night when they can visit us."

Violet looked up from the paper she was cutting. "Gloria, those flowers remind me of the flowers on your great-grandmother's bracelet. The one we saw last night."

"You're right," Gloria said. "Maybe looking at it will give us some more ideas for the patterns on the tissue paper. I'm going to get it." Gloria left the dining room and walked through the kitchen to the altar on the back porch.

A moment later she came running back in. "The bracelet!" she cried. "It's gone!"

Add to Your
Boxcar Children Collection
with New Books and Sets!

The first twelve books are now available in
three individual boxed sets!

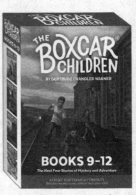

978-0-8075-0854-1 · US $24.99   978-0-8075-0857-2 · US $24.99   978-0-8075-0840-4 · US $24.99

The Boxcar Children Bookshelf includes the first twelve
books, a bookmark with complete title checklist,
and a poster with activities.

978-0-8075-0855-8 · US $69.99

The Boxcar Children 20-Book Set includes Gertrude
Chandler Warner's original nineteen books,
plus an all-new activity book, stickers,
and a magnifying glass!

978-0-8075-0847-3 · US $132.81

THE BOXCAR CHILDREN®

GREAT ADVENTURE

An Exciting 5-Book Miniseries

**Henry, Jessie, Violet, and Benny Alden
are on a secret mission that takes
them around the world!**

When Violet finds a turtle statue that nobody's seen
before in an old trunk at home, the children are on the
case! The clue turns out to be an invitation to the
Reddimus Society, a secret guild dedicated to returning
lost treasures to where they belong.

Now the Aldens must take the statue and six mysterious
boxes across the country to deliver them safely—and keep
them out of the hands of the Reddimus Society's enemies.
It's just the beginning of
the Boxcar Children's
most amazing
adventure yet!

JOURNEY ON A RUNAWAY TRAIN
Created by Gertrude Chandler Warner

HC 978-0-8075-0695-0
PB 978-0-8075-0696-7

THE CLUE IN THE PAPYRUS SCROLL
Created by Gertrude Chandler Warner

HC 978-0-8075-0698-1
PB 978-0-8075-0699-8

THE DETOUR OF THE ELEPHANTS
Created by Gertrude Chandler Warner

HC 978-0-8075-0684-4
PB 978-0-8075-0685-1

THE SHACKLETON SABOTAGE
Created by Gertrude Chandler Warner

HC 978-0-8075-0687-5
PB 978-0-8075-0688-2

THE KHIPU AND THE FINAL KEY
Created by Gertrude Chandler Warner

HC 978-0-8075-0681-3
PB 978-0-8075-0682-0

THE COMPLETE FIVE-BOOK MINISERIES
Created by Gertrude Chandler Warner

Also available as a boxed set!
978-0-8075-0693-6 · $34.

Hardcover US $12.99 · Paperback US $6.99

GERTRUDE CHANDLER WARNER discovered when she was teaching that many readers who like an exciting story could find no books that were both easy and fun to read. She decided to try to meet this need, and her first book, *The Boxcar Children*, quickly proved she had succeeded.

Miss Warner drew on her own experiences to write the mystery. As a child she spent hours watching trains go by on the tracks opposite her family home. She often dreamed about what it would be like to set up housekeeping in a caboose or freight car—the situation the Alden children find themselves in.

While the mystery element is central to each of Miss Warner's books, she never thought of them as strictly juvenile mysteries. She liked to stress the Aldens' independence and resourcefulness and their solid New England devotion to using up and making do. The Aldens go about most of their adventures with as little adult supervision as possible— something else that delights young readers.

Miss Warner lived in Putnam, Connecticut, until her death in 1979. During her lifetime, she received hundreds of letters from girls and boys telling her how much they liked her books.